Bilingual Books Collection

California Immigrant Alliance Project

Funded by
The California State Library

RIVERSIDE
PUBLIC LIBRARY

Bomberos al rescate
Firefighters to the Rescue

Alana Olsen

traducido por / translated by
Eida de la Vega

ilustrado por / illustrated by
Anita Morra

press.

New York

Published in 2017 by The Rosen Publishing Group, Inc.
29 East 21st Street, New York, NY 10010

First Edition

Translator: Eida de la Vega
Editorial Director, Spanish: Nathalie Beullens-Maoui
Editor, English: Caitie McAneney
Book Design: Michael Flynn
Illustrator: Anita Morra

Cataloging-in-Publication Data

Names: Olsen, Alana, author.
Title: Firefighters to the rescue = Bomberos al rescate / Alana Olsen.
Description: New York : PowerKids Press, [2017] | Series: Community helpers = Trabajadores de la comunidad
Identifiers: ISBN 9781499430363 (library bound book)
Subjects: LCSH: Fire fighters–Juvenile literature. | Fire
  extinction–Juvenile literature.
Classification: LCC HD8039.F5 O47 2017 | DDC 363.37092–dc23

Manufactured in the United States of America

CPSIA Compliance Information: Batch #BW17PK: For Further Information contact Rosen Publishing, New York, New York at 1-800-237-9932

Contenido

Contents

Mi tío es bombero. ¡Le encanta su trabajo!

My uncle is a firefighter. He loves his job!

4

Mi tío me lleva a la estación de bomberos.

My uncle takes me to the firehouse.

Yo quiero aprender acerca
de su trabajo.

I want to learn about his job.

7

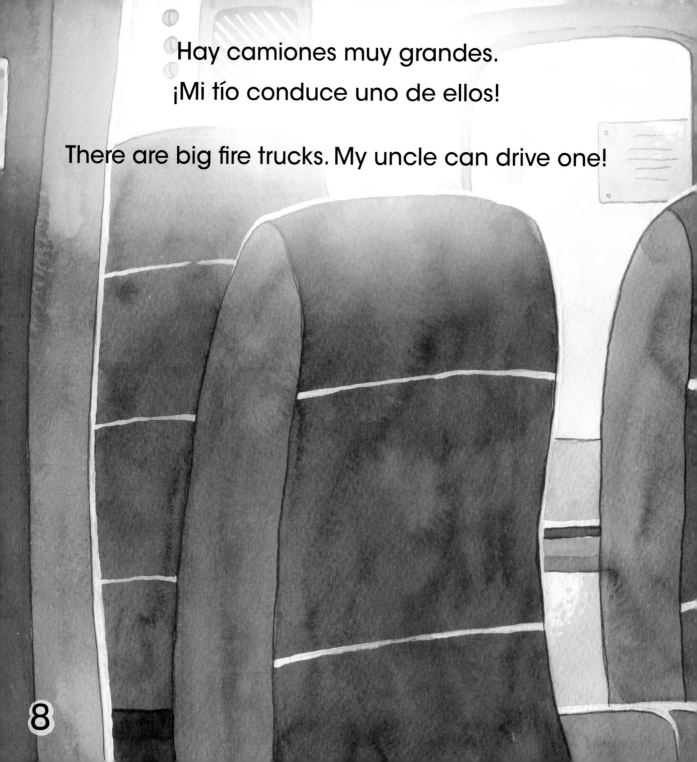

Hay camiones muy grandes.
¡Mi tío conduce uno de ellos!

There are big fire trucks. My uncle can drive one!

8

9

Todos los camiones de
bomberos tienen escaleras.

Each fire truck has ladders.

Las escaleras ayudan a los bomberos a entrar en los edificios altos.

Ladders help firefighters enter tall buildings.

Este camión de bomberos tiene una manguera.

This fire truck has a hose on it.

La manguera echa agua para apagar el fuego.

It sprays water to put out fires.

Conozco a muchos bomberos. ¡Son todos muy simpáticos!

I meet many firefighters.
They are all very nice!

Los trajes de los bomberos
los protegen de las llamas.

Firefighters' clothes keep
them safe from flames.

16

Mi tío deja que me pruebe su casco y su chaqueta.

My uncle lets me try on his hat and coat.

Mi tío recibe una llamada.

Hay un incendio en una casa.

My uncle gets a call. There's a house fire.

Todos los bomberos se preparan.

The other firefighters get ready.

19

Estoy preocupada por el incendio de la casa.
Mi tío dice que los bomberos lo apagaron.

I'm worried about the house fire. My uncle
says the firefighters put it out.

21

Yo quiero algún día ser bombero.

I want to be a firefighter someday.

¡Así también podré ayudar a
mis amigos y a mis vecinos!

Then I can help my friends
and neighbors, too!

Palabras que debes aprender
Words to Know

(la) estación de
bomberos
firehouse

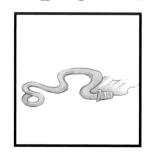

(la) manguera
hose

(la) escalera
ladder

Índice / Index